Tooter's
Stinky Wish

by Brian Cretney • Illustrated by Peggy Collins

Fitzhenry & Whiteside

Published in Canada by Fitzhenry & Whiteside, 195 Allstate Parkway, Markham, Ontario L3R 4T8

Published in the United States by Fitzhenry & Whiteside, 311 Washington Street, Brighton, Massachusetts 02135

www.fitzhenry.ca   godwit@fitzhenry.ca

10 9 8 7 6 5 4 3 2 1

Library and Archives Canada Cataloguing in Publication
Cretney, Brian, 1975-
Tooter's stinky wish / Brian Cretney, Peggy Collins.
ISBN 978-1-55455-165-1
I. Collins, Peggy II. Title.
PS8605.R465T66 2011   jC813'.6   C2011-901471-8

Publisher Cataloging-in-Publication Data (U.S)
Cretney, Brian.
Tooter's Stinky Wish / Brian Cretney ; Peggy Collins.
[32] p. : col. ill. ; 21.59 x 27.94 cm.
Summary: Tooter is a skunk that just can't stink. He tries everything from scientific experiments to self-help manuals.
In despair, he wishes on an evening star. A small bug overhears his wish and takes him on a journey of discovery where Tooter learns
the value of perspective, perseverance, and patience. And when Fox tries to turn Tooter into a midnight snack, Tooter discovers that
his new friend packs a powerful stinky punch of his own.
ISBN: 978-1-55455-165-1
1. Animals – Juvenile fiction. 2. Skunks – Juvenile fiction. 3. Friendship – Juvenile fiction. I. Collins, Peggy. II. Title.
[E] dc22   PZ10.3C747To 2011

Fitzhenry & Whiteside acknowledges with thanks the Canada Council for the Arts, and the Ontario Arts Council
for their support of our publishing program. We acknowledge the financial support of the Government of Canada through the
Book Publishing Industry Development Program (BPIDP) for our publishing activities.

Brian Cretney is at www.bc4books.com • Peggy Collins is at www.peggysillustration.com
Cover and interior design by Kerry Designs
Cover image by Peggy Collins

Printed by Sheck Wah Tong, in Hong Kong, China, April 2011, Job # 53047.

To the memory of my beloved grandfather, J. Boyd Nicholson,

whose example inspires me still. — B.C.

To my own little tooters, Mo and Zaley—

may all your wishes come true. — P.C.

THE SKUNK

Tooter was no ordinary skunk.
Sure, he looked like one:
Black fur. White stripe. Long tail.

But Tooter didn't stink like an ordinary skunk.
In fact, Tooter didn't stink at all—which *really*
stinks if you happen to be a skunk.

"Why do I have to be the only
skunk in the whole world that
can't spray?" he sighed.

Tooter tried everything to be like the other skunks.

He researched.

But when Jack scared Tooter...

...nothing happened.

Tooter changed his diet.

But when Prunella pulled one of her pranks...

...nothing happened.

And Tooter's experiments didn't help much either.

Finally, Tooter wished upon a shooting star. "Here goes nothing," he murmured.

I wish to stink, I wish to spray. I wish to scare some beast away.

But when he tried to spray a baby mouse...nothing.
"Who-o-o-ever heard of a stinkless skunk?" scowled Owl.

All the night animals laughed as Tooter scurried away into the gloomy shadows of the forest.

"It's *useless*," he told himself. "I'll never stink like a real skunk. I GIVE UP!"

"So soon?" came a voice.

Tooter stopped and looked around. But he saw no one.

"Down here," the voice called again. There, perched on a blade of grass, was a tiny bug.

"Perhaps I can help," offered the bug.

"Perhaps *not*," muttered Tooter as he started to walk away.

"You might be surprised," said the bug as he hopped onto Tooter's tail. "Let me show you something."

"Go ahead and touch the moon," said the bug.

Tooter looked up. "Listen, Bug. I'm just a skunk, not an *astronaut*."

To prove his point, Tooter jumped. And jumped. And jumped some more.

"There you have it," said Tooter. "A skunk who can't spray AND who can't touch the moon. Thanks for your help."

"Not *that* moon," the bug said with a smile.
Tooter looked down. And then he understood.

"Look at me! I'm floating on the moon!" he exclaimed.

Together, Tooter and the bug splashed the moon. They drank the moon. They even belly-flopped the moon.

"Lesson one: Perspective," said the bug. "Sometimes you need to change the way you look at problems."

The waters became chilly.

"Time to dry off," said the bug. "And I know the perfect place."

"Up we go!" chirped the bug.

"Listen, Bug. I'm just a skunk, not a *mountain goat*," said Tooter.

And to show what a poor climber he was, Tooter started up the path.
He climbed. And climbed. And climbed some more.

"Almost there..." said the bug.

When they finally reached the top, Tooter looked at the village below.

He couldn't believe his eyes.

"Wow! I've never seen anything like *this* before," he said.

"Lesson two: Perseverance," said the bug. "You never know what joys you'll miss if you give up too soon."

Tooter sat on the edge of the cliff, watching the lights flicker below.
"It looks like a great big birthday cake!"

"Then make a wish and blow out the candles," said the bug.

"Very funny," Tooter replied, "but I'm just a skunk, not a *magician*. Watch this."

Then he drew in a deep breath and blew as hard as he could.

I wish to stink, I wish to spray.
I wish to scare some beast away.

Not a single light went out.

So they waited. And waited.

And waited some more.

One by one, all the lights went out as the village fell fast asleep.

"Lesson three: Patience," said the bug. "Some things can't be rushed. They'll happen in their own time."

Tooter looked up at the stars. "But I've waited my whole life—
and nothing's happened! I'm still a stinkless skunk!"

Bug whispered, "You have one more lesson to learn, my friend.
And I have a feeling that lesson is just around the corner..."

"Well, well! So *you're* the stinkless skunk. I've heard so much about you," said the fox, his eyes glinting in the moonlight.

"I've been hoping to eat you—I mean *meet* you—for a long time!"

He licked his hairy lips.

"Here it is," whispered the bug. "Your final lesson. Now turn around and lift your tail."

"But listen, Bug! I'm just a skunk…"

"Exactly!" said the bug.

Trembling, Tooter lifted his tail high into the air. He dug his feet firmly into the earth. He could hear his heart thumping in his chest like a drum.

Then, to Tooter's surprise…

...that very tiny bug let out an *enormous*

"Your final lesson: Partnership," announced the bug. "Some dreams come true with the help of a friend...

"...especially if that friend is a *stink* bug!"

And Tooter has been
dreaming ever since.

After all...

...Tooter, you see, is no ordinary skunk.

I Stink, Therefore I Am

The Skunk:

A skunk sprays its stinky oil through two grape-sized glands found at the base of its tail. You might think a skunk would use this special weapon as often as possible. After all, it only needs 1.5 ml (1/2 teaspoon) of its oil to be smelled as far as 1.6 kilometres away. That's about the length of 127 lined-up school buses! However, skunks only have enough scent for five or six sprays. When their oil is all gone, they must wait up to ten days for their scent glands to build up a fresh supply. So a skunk will only use its spray as a last resort after trying other scare tactics such as hissing, foot stamping, and then finally doing a handstand with its tail high in the air to make it look larger than it actually is.

The Stink Bug:

It really is amazing: a bug the size of a grown-up's fingernail can stink up to 1.5 metres (5 feet) away! That might not sound like a lot, but for someone your size, it would be the same as your smelly feet's odour reaching the back of a 70-kid line-up! Unlike the skunk, though, the stink bug's odour can be washed away with just water and soap. It's also amazing how this little critter eats. Stink bugs do not have mouths. Instead, they have straw-like beaks called "rostrums" attached to their heads. They stick their rostrums into plants in order to suck up their sap. Some stink bugs don't stop at plants to get their daily juice intake: some even stab their rostrums right into other insects, like slow moving caterpillars, and suck up their body juices as well!

Play the "Aim Game."

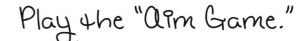

Pretend to be a skunk! Go outside with a measuring tape, a piece of chalk, a spray/squirt bottle, and your parents' permission. Follow these steps:

1. Because skunks can aim extremely well up to 3 metres (10 feet) away, measure that distance from a wall. Draw a line on your driveway with your chalk.
2. With the chalk, draw a pair of small eyes on the wall (the size of two pennies). Skunks like to aim for the predator's eyes because the spray blinds the animal long enough for the skunk to get away.
3. Now, stand on your line, facing away from the wall. Hold your squirt gun in your hand.
4. On the count of three, quickly turn around and try to spray the eyes as if your life depended on it. Remember, you only get five or six squirts, just like a skunk. Not as easy as you might think, is it?

Your Nose Knows.

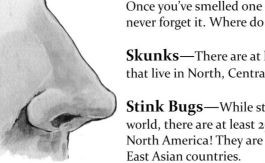

Once you've smelled one of these stinkers, you'll never forget it. Where do they live?

Skunks—There are at least 13 kinds of skunks that live in North, Central and South America.

Stink Bugs—While stink bugs live all over the world, there are at least 250 different kinds of stink bugs in North America! They are believed to have first come from East Asian countries.

For more stinky information and activities, visit Tooter's website at www.fitzhenry.ca/tooter

Stink-Be-Gone!

Here is a simple, safe way to get rid of that nasty odour if someone has been sprayed by a skunk.

- Prepare a warm bath and add a mixture of: 1 litre (4 cups) of white vinegar, 51 grams (1/4 cup) of baking soda, and 4.5 grams (1 teaspoon) of dish detergent. These counteract the natural oils in the skunk's spray.

- Note: 3% hydrogen peroxide can be used in place of white vinegar; however, the peroxide may bleach clothes and your carpet.

P.S. While some think tomato juice helps, it appears to only mask the smell for a little while.

Other Animals That Raise a Stink

Giant Petrel:	Aims a straight stream of vomit at attackers.
Millipede:	While not poisonous to humans, certain millipedes can kill a mouse with their smell alone!
Hooker's Sea Lion:	Eats so much fish, its breath smells horrible.
Lemur (male):	He wipes smelly liquid from his wrist and shoulder glands all over his tail, and then waves his tail at his lemur opponent. Their stink fights can last up to one hour!
Vulture:	This bird smothers its legs and feet with dung to keep them cool.

Draw Tooter!

1. Draw three ovals.
2. Add arms, legs, ears, and a nose.
3. Draw his eyes, a stripe down his nose, and a tuft of hair on his head. Don't forget the tail!
4. Colour him in black, leaving a white patch on his tummy and a white stripe down his face and his tail (of course)!

Skunk Prints

Draw a Stink Bug!

1. Draw a long, narrow oval.
2. Add a line across the top third of the oval for his mouth and a long skinny triangle down each side for his armour.
3. Add eyes, antennae, and legs.
4. Give him a smile, googly eyes and four more legs/arms—two on each side.
5. Finish off his armour by drawing a line down his middle and three more lines across his tummy.